SPACE TAXI
THE GALACTIC B.U.R.P.

By Wendy Mass and Michael Brawer

Ⓛ Ⓑ

LITTLE, BROWN AND COMPANY
New York   Boston

Copyright © 2016 by Wendy Mass and Michael Brawer
Illustrations by Keith Frawley, based on the art of Elise Gravel

Little, Brown and Company

Hachette Book Group
1290 Avenue of the Americas, New York, NY 10104
Visit us at lb-kids.com

Little, Brown and Company is a division of Hachette Book Group, Inc.
The Little, Brown name and logo are trademarks of Hachette Book Group, Inc.

The publisher is not responsible for websites (or their content) that are not owned by the publisher.

First Edition: May 2016

Library of Congress Cataloging-in-Publication Data

Mass, Wendy, 1967– author.
The galactic B.U.R.P. / by Wendy Mass and Michael Brawer ; illustrations by Keith Frawley ; based on the art of Elise Gravel. — First edition.
pages ; cm. — (Space taxi ; 4)
Summary: While trying to stop thieves from getting the last known canisantha plant for an unknown purpose, eight-year-old Intergalactic Security Force deputy Archie is mistaken for someone very important and directed by his trainer, Pockets the cat, to go on a spy mission aboard a B.U.R.P. ship.
ISBN 978-0-316-24331-5 (hardcover) — ISBN 978-0-316-24330-8 (paperback)—
ISBN 978-0-316-24329-2 (ebook) —ISBN 978-0-316-24332-2 (library edition ebook)
[1. Spies—Fiction. 2. Criminals—Fiction. 3. Rare plants—Fiction. 4. Interplanetary voyages—Fiction. 5. Adventure and adventurers—Fiction. 6. Fathers and sons—Fiction. 7. Science fiction.]
I. Brawer, Michael, author. II. Frawley, Keith, illustrator. III. Title.
PZ7.M42355Gal 2015
[Fic]—dc23
2015004572

HC: 10 9 8 7 6 5 4 3 2 1
PB: 10 9 8 7 6 5 4 3 2

LSC-C

Printed in the United States of America

To the amazing young readers of
Sparta, New Jersey:
Thank you all for coming along
for the ride.

CONTENTS

Chapter One:
Training Day

"Faster, Archie, faster!" Pockets shouts as I get closer. "Pretend a hippoctopus from Omega 9 is chasing you. He thinks you're dinner!"

Sneakers pounding on the sidewalk, I finally turn the corner and reach the courtyard behind our apartment building. I lean against the brick wall, panting. Pockets steps out from behind the large tree he was using as cover. Even though it's rare to find anyone back here besides me and my sister, Penny, it's best to be careful. No one can know that Pockets is actually a super intergalactic crime fighter and not just our giant, fluffy pet cat who sheds a lot and sleeps even more. He clicks his stopwatch and shakes his head in disapproval.

"What...*pant pant*...is a hippoctopus?" I ask. "Is that like a cross between a hippo...*pant*...and an octopus?"

Pockets's eyes dart left and right. When he's completely sure we're alone, he says, "Exactly. Only bigger, smellier, and with more arms. Now, let's go twice more around the building, this time backward."

I shake my head. "I need a break. I've been running for an hour straight while alternating between bouncing a tennis ball and jumping rope. I don't know if you've tried it, but it's pretty much impossible to do without looking totally ridiculous." In fact, my downstairs neighbor, Mr. Goldblatt, shouted *Oy vey!* when I ran/jumped/bounced by for the fifth time while he was walking his dog. He says that to me and my sister, Penny, a lot, usually while shaking his head in disbelief at the same time. He's cranky, but he's really nice, too. After I told him that Dad had taken me to Barney's Bagels and Schmear, Mr. Goldblatt was the one who explained that *schmear* can actually mean two things—the act of coating the bagel with a spread, such as cream cheese, or the cream cheese itself. Like THAT'S not confusing! I know he'd love to hear that aliens are real and that I've actually been on other planets, but Dad and I have to keep the space taxi thing—and especially our jobs as Intergalactic Security Force deputies—a secret.

"Part of your training is to improve your hand-eye coordination and balance," Pockets says. "As an ISF deputy, you have to be quick on your feet and ready to react in the blink of an eye." He tucks his stopwatch into one of the endlessly deep pockets hidden in his fur and then pulls out two pairs of sunglasses. He tosses me a pair and sticks the other on his face. For a cat, he can rock a pair of sunglasses like no one else I know.

"All right, you've earned a rest," he says. "You're actually pretty fast for a human boy."

I gratefully drop the rope and ball at my feet and take a long sip from my water bottle. "Are humans known for being slow?" I ask. "I mean, compared to people on other planets?"

"They are slower than approximately 9,356,110 other species."

"Wow, that's pretty slow."

Pockets shrugs. "Like everything, it's all in the way you look at it. You're also faster than at least sixteen billion species, if that makes you feel any better."

"It does, a little," I admit. "Let's hope I'm on one of *those* planets when something big and smelly with more than eight arms wants to eat me for dinner." I slip on my glasses. "So, what are these for? It's not very sunny out." The glasses make the courtyard look only a tiny bit darker.

"Slide your hand around the frame on the left until you feel a little switch," he instructs. "Then push it toward you."

I follow his instructions, and the lenses flicker. I blink in surprise. Instead of seeing Pockets next to the tree, which is what I'd been looking at, all I see is myself, standing in front of the wall. I turn my head from side to side, but the view doesn't change. It's like I'm frozen in place. That's weird! Then Pockets says, "I'm going to turn my head now," and suddenly I can see not only myself but also the sides of the building, the small laundry room window above my

head, and the jump rope in a heap on the ground. "I get it!" I say excitedly. "I'm seeing what *you're* seeing!"

"Correct. Now push the switch in the opposite direction and I will see what *you* see."

I push the switch. My view returns to normal. I walk in a circle around Pockets and ask, "Do you see yourself now?"

He grins and puts a paw on his hip. "I'm one handsome cat, aren't I? I don't believe I've ever seen my own rump before."

I giggle at the word *rump*. "Not sure you'll win any beauty contests, but you're all right as far as giant talking cats go." We both switch our glasses back to the regular setting.

Pockets reaches into his pocket and pulls out a wireless earpiece. I've seen him use one to talk long-distance with his dad, but I've never seen it up close. He holds out the tiny device and I grab it. "My own earpiece?" I ask, sticking it in my ear before he can change his mind. *"Oooohh!"*

It instantly molds to the shape of my earlobe and is so small I doubt anyone could see it unless they were peering into my ear from an inch away, which would be weird. "It tickles! Do I get to keep it?"

"For now," he says, sticking one in his own ear. "We will practice using them so we'll be able to communicate if we get separated on a mission. Hopefully, we won't have to worry about that, of course."

"Hey, I did okay on my own on our last mission, right? I rescued the princess by myself."

Pockets clears his throat. "Well, you may have had a *little* help."

Before I can argue, Mr. Goldblatt's tiny black pug, Luna, slowly trots into the courtyard, her leash trailing behind her.

Luna is old and half-blind, so I guess Mr. Goldblatt isn't worried about her running away before he catches up. She's still sharp enough to spot the yellow tennis ball at my feet, though, and pounces on it.

I bend down to pet her. "Hey there, Luna, old girl. How are you doing?" In response, she slobbers all over the ball. A little drool gets on my ankle and drips into my sock, but I don't mind.

"Don't make any sudden moves," a low, deep voice hisses in my ear.

Chapter Two:
The Beast

I spin around but don't see anyone. And hey, where did Pockets go? The voice comes again. "What did I say about sudden moves! She's going to see me!"

"Who is this?" I say, straightening up. "Where are you?"

"It's *me*, obviously!" Pockets says in his normal voice.

I laugh and my hand goes up to my earpiece. I'd forgotten about it already! "It really feels like you're inside my head," I shout. "So you can hear me, too?"

"Of course I can hear you! Wouldn't be much of a communication device if it only went one way. And no need to shout."

"Okay, okay, I get it." I look behind the tree where he'd been hiding earlier, but I only find a squirrel picking apart an acorn. "Where are you?"

"Look up!"

The glasses help shade my eyes from the setting sun as I peer up into the branches. I spot Pockets's white tail swishing through the leaves about halfway up. "What are you doing up there?" I ask.

"Hiding from that beast," he replies.

I laugh. "Old Luna? She wouldn't hurt a fly. Or a cat, as the case may be." On hearing her name, Luna barks and rolls over, the ball tucked under one paw.

A few leaves flutter to the ground next to us. Then more leaves. Pockets is climbing higher.

"C'mon, Pockets, don't be scared," I tell him. "You're ten times the size of this dog. If you're really scared, you can put up a force field like you did when you didn't want to go to the groomer to get a haircut."

"Dogs are tricky," he insists. "It would get through somehow, I'm certain."

I start to tell him that Luna can barely

finish lunch without falling asleep, much less summon the strength to break through a force field, but he's not listening. "You should climb up here, too, Archie," he says. "Scaling trees is good practice. In fact, it's on our list for tomorrow."

I shake my head. "The last time I was in a tree, I met you! That turned out to be a pretty good tree. I'm sure this one would just be a disappointment after that one."

He starts to reply, but another, deeper, voice cuts into my earpiece. "Pilarbing? Can you hear me?"

"I can hear you, Father," Pockets says after settling himself directly on top of the tree. He looks like the world's largest Christmas tree ornament!

"Hi, Mr. Catapolitus!" I shout. "It's Archie."

"Young Morningstar?" the chief of the ISF asks. "What are you doing on this communication channel? And why are you shouting?"

Pockets replies for me. "We are testing out the earpieces, Father. I can switch to a private line if you prefer."

"No, this call concerns Archie, too."

"A new mission?" I ask. I start to jump up and down but catch myself. I *am* almost nine, after all.

"Maybe," he says. "But right now we have a mystery on our hands. We are tracking a very unusual break-in. The thieves are known agents of B.U.R.P. We cannot think of why the sneakiest criminal organization in the universe would take the risk, though. Pilarbing, you're the best officer we have when it comes to figuring out B.U.R.P.'s

17

motives. I'm sending the information to your handheld right now. Let me know when the data arrives."

"Er...I can't do that right now, sir. I'm a bit busy gripping a tree trunk."

"Well, climb down, then."

Pockets shifts his weight to balance better. A leaf lands on Luna's nose, and she cranes her neck to see where it came from. She sniffs at the air, then loses interest and stops to scratch an itch with her hind leg.

"That might be a while," Pockets says, sending more leaves fluttering down as his tail twitches crazily.

"Why?" his father asks. Then his words speed up. "Are you in danger?"

"Yes," Pockets replies.

"No," I reply at the same time.

"Explain," the chief demands.

"There is a huge dog at the base of the tree," Pockets says.

"It is a tiny dog," I argue. "Barely the size of a loaf of bread."

Pockets's dad is silent. All I hear is heavy breathing.

"Sir?" I ask. "Are you still there?"

Then, his voice quivering, Pockets's dad asks, "Does the beast have long, pointy teeth?"

"Yes," Pockets says hurriedly.

I glance down at Luna, who is currently licking my calf. "No, sir," I reply. "Her teeth are small and stubby, like kernels of corn. Trust me, Pockets has stood up to the biggest, baddest criminals in the universe and won. This little dog wouldn't hurt any—"

But the chief ignores me. "Pilarbing!" he shouts. "I want you to remain calm and don't let go of that tree! Archie, I need you to use all your ISF deputy skills to protect my firstborn, my only son, my pride and joy. Do I need to fly out there? I can be there by morning."

I sigh. "I got this, Chief. No worries." I bend down and scoop Luna under one arm. She licks my face. As I head out of the courtyard, I hear Pockets say, "Stay with me, Daddy."

"Always, son."

As Mr. Goldblatt would say, *"Oy vey!"*

Chapter Three:
Plants Versus Pockets

It took nearly an hour to convince Pockets to come down from the tree. I wound up missing baseball practice, which I think Pockets was actually glad about. He had promised to come with me, even though he said watching humans play baseball is worse than watching Aniwerps play roly-poly-poppy, whatever THAT is! Instead, I spent the afternoon yelling up into a tree. It was Penny's idea to leave a can of tuna fish open on the ground. She's pretty smart for a three-year-old. Pockets climbed right down, gobbled it up, and announced (once Penny left to play on the swings) that he was ready to get to work on solving the mystery. He would need privacy and access to plenty of food and water, and some soft music would be nice.

He has been shut inside my bedroom closet ever since, having turned it into his own mini ISF headquarters. He tossed all my stuff out of the closet and shoved in three different computers and two printers, one of which makes 3-D objects instead

of just printing out paper! Once he solves his mystery, I plan on asking if I can use the 3-D printer to make a LEGO piece to replace the foot missing from my LEGO dinosaur. Penny took the foot last month because it was purple. Personally, I think she ate it. But if it ever comes out the other end, I definitely don't want it back.

Every few hours Pockets pops his head out, rubs his eyes with the back of his paw, and ducks back in. Dad and I keep offering to help, but he turns us down. I think he's a little embarrassed about his freakout over tiny, harmless Luna and wants to prove he can do this on his own. Finally, I tell him I'm going to bed.

The *click-clack* of paws pounding on a keyboard (not to mention the paper crumpling and the muttering) makes sleeping impossible.

"Any chance of stopping for the night?" I call out. "Running around the block a million times tires a kid out."

The closet door creaks open and Pockets appears. His eyes are red and his ears are droopy. "This isn't any fun for me, either," he says. "Between this case and that horrid beast, I've missed seven naps today."

I sit up in bed. "Can you just tell me what you're looking for in there?"

He leaps onto the bed. "Fine. An attempted robbery was reported at a greenhouse on Alpha 43. This greenhouse contains a collection of the rarest plants in the universe and is very well guarded. The thieves toppled all the plants and mixed them up, so no one knows exactly what they were after. The only good news is that one of the guards grabbed the plant from the thieves before their daring escape through the sewer system. So now the ISF knows what the plant looks like, but not its name."

"Why would someone want to steal a plant?" Honestly, I'd hoped the mission would have been more exciting. A stolen plant that wasn't even really stolen? BORING!

Pockets yawns. "Many reasons, I suppose. You can make medicines out of some plants. Or maybe it has pretty flowers and they simply want it for their own garden. Perhaps they want to collect or sell it because it is rare. When an object is the only one of its kind, its value grows."

I think for a minute. "If they knew chances were good that they'd get caught, they must have wanted that one plant pretty bad."

"Exactly," Pockets says. "That's why the ISF is worried. If a group like B.U.R.P. is willing to take a big risk for something that seems to offer a very small reward, we must not be seeing the whole picture. I've been trying to find some information about the plant, but no luck so far. I'm also monitoring all the local police reports to see if any other plants have been reported stolen recently." Pockets yawns. "Maybe just a short nap." He curls his tail around his body, and before I can even lie down again, he's purring loudly, probably dreaming of mice swimming in a bowl of tuna fish.

Beep! Beep! Beep! Pockets and I bolt upright. The room is still dark, and Dad is not working tonight. So why is my alarm going off?

Pockets springs off the bed and into the closet. It takes me a few seconds to realize it's not my alarm going off at all. It's his computer.

He returns with a sheet of paper and holds it up, triumphant. "Got it! And we can cross off the idea that someone is after the plant because it's pretty."

He flicks his paw, but instead of his claws coming out, a little beam of light shines onto the page. That's a neat trick! The picture shows a small patch of yellow-brown weeds, like straw almost, but thicker, and droopy. Under the picture are these words:

Canisantha, NE, C-NP, D-TBD

"What do all those letters mean?" I ask.

"*NE* stands for *nearly extinct*," he says. "*Extinct* means when a type of plant or animal is no longer around anymore."

I roll my eyes. "I know what *extinct* means."

"How do I know what they teach in third grade on your planet?"

"Just go on."

"*C-NP* means *contact not poisonous*," he says. "There are no oils on the leaves that would harm your skin, the way poison ivy and poison oak can. *D-TBD* means that the effects of digesting the plant are *to be determined*. Which really means tests haven't been done on it."

I glance down at the picture again. I sure wouldn't want to eat that. "All right, then," I say, snuggling under my blanket. "Case closed. See ya tomorrow."

"Not so fast. This morning we worked on some physical drills; now let's do some brain training. If we want to catch the people trying to steal canisantha, what should we do?"

I'm tempted to say *Just let them have*

it—it's only a plant, but I'm pretty sure that's not the correct answer. "I don't know," I tell him instead, which isn't much better. "It's extinct anyway, right?"

"It's only *nearly* extinct," he reminds me. "That means it exists somewhere, only in very tiny amounts. I'm going to research where to find canisantha in the wild. Then in the morning we'll saddle up the space taxi and wrangle us a couple of plant thieves."

"Why are you talking like a cowboy?" I mumble as I doze off. I hear him say something about watching movies about the Old West on TV with Dad, but that's all I remember until I hear a bloodcurdling *screeeeech!*

Once again, I bolt upright, my heart

pounding this time. More yowling and screeching. I jump out of bed. "Pockets?" I open the closet door, but he's not in there. "Pockets! Where are you?"

"*Yooowl . . . eeeekkk . . . meeeooowww!*"

I drop to the floor next to the bed and press my cheek to the rug. At first I can't see anything in the dark, but then Pockets's eyes glint and I spot him. At that moment, Mom, Dad, and Penny run into the room.

"What's going on?" Dad asks, flipping on the light switch. "Is everything all right?"

Penny is wrapped around Mom's leg, clutching her stuffed dragon and sucking her thumb. She still does that only when she's really scared.

"Everything's fine," I tell them. "I mean, Pockets is upset about something, but I don't know what. Maybe he had a bad dream?"

From beneath the bed, Pockets whimpers. Since Penny's in the room, he can't tell us anything. I notice something I wasn't able to see in the dark—a newly balled-up piece of paper just outside the closet door. The others set about trying to get Pockets to come out while I unfold the paper. It has only one sentence printed on it:

The last remaining canisantha plant in the universe grows on the highest peak of planet Canis.

I pull Dad aside and whisper, "I think this is where our next mission will be. But I don't know why Pockets is so freaked out."

Dad looks down at the paper. "I know why," he says. "*Canis* is the word scientists give to the group of animals that includes the common dog."

"So you're saying that *planet Canis* means...*dog planet*?"

Dad nods. "'Fraid so."

"*Oy vey!*" I exclaim.

Dad looks at the shaking Pockets and says, "You can say *that* again!"

CHAPTER FOUR:
No Way, No How

"Good morning, Minerva," Dad says into the com system as he adjusts his rearview mirror. "Morningstar and son checking in."

"Always nice to hear from you," Minerva says cheerily, "but I don't have you on the schedule for today."

"The ISF is sending us out on a mission," Dad replies. "I will plug in our destination now." He presses a button on the dash, and the keyboard pops out. But instead of typing in the data, he turns the keyboard in my direction.

"Here's the information, Archie," he says, handing me a slip of paper. "You should learn how to do this." Dad hasn't let me touch anything on the dashboard yet! I eagerly begin inputting the information.

Destination: planet Canis in the Canis Major dwarf galaxy

Takeoff: 8:00 a.m.

Arrival: approx. 1:00 p.m.

Time and date of return: unknown

Passengers: Salazar Morningstar, Archie Morningstar, Agent Pilarbing

Fangorious Catapolitus, aka Pockets
the cat

    Systems: checked and ready

    Weather: partly cloudy

I'm not the world's best typist, so it takes me a lot longer than it would have taken him.

"Good job," Dad says, pushing the keyboard back in. Pleased, I slide my space map out of its case so I'll be ready as soon as we get the all clear from Minerva. But when she does come back on the com line, she's laughing so hard she can't speak. And let me tell you, the sound of a mouse laughing isn't all that pleasant. It's high-pitched and whiny and hurts my ears. "There is no way you're telling me that cat is going to planet Canis," she finally says. "No way, no how."

I almost tell her that's exactly what Pockets said last night when Dad told him we would be leaving early in the morning, but I feel like I have to defend him. "He *is* going," I insist.

"Then where is he?" she asks.

"He's coming," I reply, glancing out the taxi's back window.

"You expect me to believe," she says, "that a cat is going to willingly travel to a planet inhabited by nothing but dogs? And I don't mean civilized dogs that walk and talk and have cities and play ball games. I mean wild dogs whose first thought when they see a cat is to chase it."

That news about the dogs being wild surprises me. I figured they were talking dogs, like Pockets is a talking cat

and Minerva is a talking mouse. "Well...
maybe not exactly *willingly*," I admit.

"Here he comes now!" Dad says. He
and I jump out of the car. Mom and Penny
are pushing Pockets in the crate that Dad
rigged together in the middle of the night.
It's like the world's largest cat carrier, but
on wheels. A regular-size cat could eas-
ily squeeze between the wooden slats, but
Pockets can only stick his paws through.

Pockets scowls at us when he's wheeled
up to the car. I know he has a lot he'd like
to say to my dad and me, but he can't say
anything in front of Penny. We only got
him into the crate in the first place because
he fell into such a deep sleep after all the
yowling and carrying-on. Dad and I were
able to slide him right in without waking

him. The motion of the crate kept him sleeping, so Mom and Penny have been rolling him up and down the block for the last hour like a baby in a stroller. Looks like he finally woke up!

"Got a lot of strange glances," Mom tells us. Penny kneels down beside the crate. Her cheeks get all puffy when she wants to say something but can't get the words out. We're used to it. Only this time, once she lets out the air, she breathes in again and says, "Bye-bye, Pockets. Please come home soon."

Mom, Dad, and I gasp. Even Pockets stops glaring at us, and his ears perk up. That is the longest sentence Penny has ever said. It may actually be the ONLY full sentence she's ever said. In fact, it was really TWO sentences! Mom's eyes fill with tears, and she bends down to pull Penny into her arms. "Oh, sweetie! I'm so proud of you! Talking like the big girl you are! And of course Pockets is coming back. Daddy's just taking him on a little ride."

Penny squirms out of Mom's arms and reaches through the slats into the crate. Pockets moves closer so she can stroke his neck. "I love you, Pockets!" she says. "You're the best pet ever!"

Of course this makes Mom fully start to cry. Dad and I may have wiped away a tear or two—I'm not gonna lie.

"We'd better get going," Dad says, patting Penny on the head. "Otherwise we'll never leave."

It takes me, Dad, *and* Mom to lift the crate into the backseat. It doesn't help that Penny and Pockets keep reaching for each other. Penny has begun listing all the ways that Pockets is the best pet—he's cute, he's cuddly, he sleeps on her bed and keeps her feet warm, his purrs sound like music, and on and on. I guess now that Penny has decided to start talking, she has no plans to ever stop!

As soon as the car door closes and Mom leads Penny away, Pockets starts yelling at us. "What do you think you're doing? I outrank you! I order you to release me and deliver me back to the apartment!"

"I knew it!" Minerva says, her laughter cackling through the com line.

"Hey," Pockets shouts at her. "I haven't seen you book a trip to MY planet!"

The idea of a mouse vacationing on a planet full of cats quiets her right down.

"Let's just focus on the job ahead," Dad

says, heading out of town toward the airfield. "We know you don't want to go, Pockets. And trust me—your father is beside himself with worry, but he knows you're the best officer for the job. He made us promise to keep you far away from any dogs. You'll stay with the taxi while Archie and I retrieve the plant."

Pockets finally settles down. "I don't have to leave the taxi?" he asks.

"That's right," Dad says.

"We can use those glasses and the earpiece you gave me yesterday," I suggest to Pockets. "That way it will be like you're there with us."

"Fine," he grumbles, pulling out his pillow. He curls up on top of it but doesn't shut his eyes.

"Ready for liftoff?" Dad asks me.

I turn back around and focus on the map. I ask it for the best route, and the map responds to my voice by filling the air over my lap with planets and stars.

"That's strange," I say, turning the map around to get a better view. "The Canis Major dwarf galaxy is right next to our Milky Way, but the trip to get there is really long and winding. And the travel time we sent Minerva said five hours. We've passed through *ten* galaxies before in less time than that."

"Yes, but there aren't any wormholes between us and Canis Major," Dad says, raising his voice over the increasing roar of the engine and the grinding sound the wings make as they come out from the sides of the taxi. "That means we can't take any shortcuts. You'll have to pay careful attention because we'll be passing through a lot of populated areas. There will be many more stars and planets than you're used to navigating around."

That sounds scary! I make sure my double seat-belt system is tight and brace myself as the front wheels lift off the ground. That first part—when half the car is flying and half is driving—still takes some getting used to.

I focus on my space map. There are so many objects floating in front of me that I can barely see the dashboard through them. "Okay," I reply, peering at it all nervously. "We'll have to exit the solar system after we pass Mars. There are a lot of asteroids flying between the orbits of Mars and Jupiter, though."

"Yup," Dad says, slowing as we approach Mars. "That's the Asteroid Belt. We can usually avoid flying through it, but sometimes the only way around is through."

I reach out with my finger and touch one of the tiny map asteroids whizzing by my face in an almost perfect circle. It's moving so fast that the words above it are hard to read. I think they're telling me the rock is one of millions zooming around this part of the solar system. Now all I have to do is make sure we avoid them all!

"Hang on, guys," I tell Dad and Pockets. "It's gonna be a bumpy ride!"

Chapter Five:
What Would Pockets Do?

For a half hour I shout out directions like: "Turn east! No, not yet...now! Okay, straight past the asteroid that looks like a giant football. Okay, slow down so the one that looks like Pockets's butt can pass in front of us. I don't want that thing getting too close!"

Pockets *harumph*s from the backseat, but Dad laughs. I think he's having fun zigging and zagging to avoid the giant rocks. My stomach's getting a little queasy, but we're almost out of the Asteroid Belt. At least there were no loop-the-loops like in the wormholes.

The rest of the trip to Canis is long, but we get to see some really cool things on the way. Right as we leave the Milky Way, Dad points out a stellar nursery where stars are starting to form. A special coating on the windshield allows us to actually see the gas and dust swirling around us, clumping together to form baby stars. I point it out to Pockets, but he only grunts at me. I don't take it personally.

"We are about to enter the atmosphere for Canis," I finally announce. Pockets springs up, hits the top of his crate, yelps, and shouts something that makes my dad say, "Young man, we don't use that kind of language in this taxi!"

"Sorry," Pockets mutters miserably. Then he swings his tail around, unhinges the end, and lasers a hole right through the side of the crate. He walks out onto the seat and stretches. "Ah, that's better," he says.

"Why didn't you just do that from the start?" I ask.

He shrugs. "What would be the point? I knew I needed to come with you. So guide us to the right mountaintop, oh keeper of the space map. Let's grab the plant before B.U.R.P. does, and then get out of Dodge."

"Dodge?" I ask, searching my map. "I don't see any planets with that name."

Dad chuckles. "It's not a planet. It's an expression from old western movies. It means 'to leave town quickly.'"

I feel a little left out of their late-night movie marathons, but truthfully, those old black-and-white movies are kinda boring. "Well, anyway, as soon as we pass that mountain over there with the snow on it, you'll see a peak with two tall trees. According to the ISF, that's where the plant grows."

Dad follows my instructions, but as soon as we approach the peak with the two trees, we all see the problem. There's nowhere to land! The whole mountaintop, including the trees, is about the size of our kitchen!

"Archie, you're going to have to go down there while the taxi hovers overhead," Pockets says. "I, of course, will remain here." He pulls out a folded ladder and begins unrolling it. "For added protection, you can use my force field device. As they taught us at the academy, if you fall, you'll bounce back up like a rubber ball."

"Seriously?" I ask. Pockets is always serious, so I turn to Dad. "You're going to let me climb out the window, in midair, and climb down this ladder?"

Dad takes a closer look out the window. "I can hover right next to that smaller tree. You won't actually be too far off the ground, so I'm okay with it if you are."

My eyes widen. "Awesome!"

While Dad gets into position, Pockets

rolls down the back window and attaches the ladder. It unfolds until the last rung dangles only a foot off the ground. "We'll get you as close as we can to the plant," he says, "so you won't have to get off the ladder. I think it's best not to step on the ground so the dogs don't pick up your scent as quickly."

I'd kind of forgotten about the dogs.

He hands me his force field pen and shows me what button to press to turn it on and off. "You'll have to enclose the whole taxi and the ladder, too," he says. "Otherwise you won't be able to grip the rope. Making such a wide field will quickly drain the battery, though, so make sure you turn it off when you land."

I nod, slipping the gadget into my back pocket.

"One more thing," Pockets says, pulling out a small pouch with a metal clip at the end. He clips it onto my belt loop and then sprays it all over with Camo-It-Now. "This will keep the plant safe and hidden."

"Cool," I say, reaching down to touch the now-invisible pouch. Yup, still there. Then I slide my space map into its silver case and sling it over my shoulder. After wishing I'd had it with me on the last planet to help me rescue a three-eyed princess, I'm never leaving it behind again!

"Ready?" Pockets asks.

"Giddyap!" I reply. It's the only cowboy phrase I know.

Dad gives me the thumbs-up and says, "Might not want to tell your mom about this one for a little while."

I grin and climb over my seat into the back. Pockets helps me get out the window and onto the top rung of the ladder. Once I have a solid grip, I activate the force field. I wave good-bye and begin the climb down. The ladder sways more than I'd like, but knowing that the force field is around me makes me feel braver. I look up at the car to see Pockets sticking his head out the window, watching. I can tell from his face that he wishes he could do this, too. That cat loves adventure.

When I reach the last rung, I undo the force field and look around. From my perch on the bottom rung, I can see a single stalk of the canisantha plant growing in a shady spot between the two trees, just out of my reach. If I tried to grab it and fell, would the dogs pounce on me? I wave up to Dad

and Pockets to tell them they need to move the taxi a few feet, but they just think I'm waving to say hello and so they wave back. Not helpful.

I swing for a few seconds and ask myself, *What would Pockets do?* He would do the best with what he had. Although in his case, with his endlessly deep pockets, he has everything! So I use what I have. I untie each end of the strap from my map case, then tie one end onto the rung of the ladder above me and the other end onto my belt loop. Now when I lean forward, I can let go of the ladder just enough to grab the plant without my hands or feet touching the ground. The plant feels rough, like bark, rather than soft like leaves. I can definitely see why no one wanted to try eating it!

Pockets told me to pull it out with the roots still attached, so I grab the stalk with both hands and tug. It doesn't budge. I yank harder and harder until it finally comes away in my hands. If I didn't know better, I would think the ground knew it was holding on to something so valuable and rare. I fumble for the invisible pouch and place the plant carefully inside it. As it drops back against my pants pocket, I remember I'd put the glasses and earpiece from Pockets in there. D'oh! I could have used those before! I put them on now and instantly hear Pockets shouting in my ear, "Get off the ladder! Let go of the rope! Hide behind the closest tree! Now!"

I don't even have time to think or ask

Why? or *What about the dogs?* I quickly untangle myself from the strap and dash toward the tree. The second I step away from the ladder, it shoots up and the taxi zooms off behind a nearby cloud.

So now I'm on the ground and the dogs could come at any second and there's nowhere to go. Pockets was right—I should have brushed up on my tree climbing!

"Hurry!" Pockets shouts. But I'm not moving fast enough. I know this because a very large, very hairy hand that definitely doesn't belong to Pockets or Dad—or, fortunately, a wild dog!—has just clamped down on my shoulder.

Chapter Six:
A Case of Mistaken Identity

I stand very still, afraid to turn and face the guy beside me. I'm thinking that maybe the dogs wouldn't have been so bad after all. I mean, dogs like me. At least Luna does. Maybe they would have wanted to play fetch or find a nice river to splash in.

Instead, I get *this* huge guy. (I can tell he's huge by the shadow he casts. He reminds me of Mr. Fitch, the first criminal I ever helped catch.)

"Stay calm, Archie," Pockets says in my ear. "If you can, switch on the glasses so I can see what you're seeing."

As soon as I make a move to lift my arm, the guy spins me around to face him. He is dressed in tight-fitting black clothes with a badge sewn onto the sleeve that says B.U.R.P. When he sees my face, his overly large green eyes (with no eyelids that I can spot!) widen in surprise. He quickly lets go of me and backs away. "Forgive me," he says. "I thought you were back at the spaceship napping after working so late last night. If you don't mind my asking, why are you wearing those strange clothes?"

"Er...um...huh?" I am not proud of them, but these are the only words I can come up with. I take this moment of confusion to turn on the glasses, though. The lenses flicker, and I know Pockets can see what I'm seeing now.

"He's a high-ranking B.U.R.P. agent!" Pockets says into my earpiece. "A big shot in the organization. He must think you are one of the other leaders' kids! Don't correct him."

"We should get you back up there," the man says. "We have the big meeting soon." He looks around. "How about I grab the plant now and be done with it? We don't really need to wait for the scientists to come down here."

He steps toward the trees. Uh-oh!

"Tell him to wait!" Pockets shouts in my

ear. "Tell him the plant is very fragile and you need an expert to handle it correctly! He can't find out that you have it already!"

I try to sound very commanding as I relay Pockets's commands. The B.U.R.P. agent grumbles a bit but steps back.

"Okay, then," I say. "Gotta go. See ya." I turn away, but he reaches out to stop me.

"I know you like your fresh air," he says, "but we must stay on schedule." He taps his watch. "Plus, you know it isn't safe out here with all the wild dogs."

It's weird that he doesn't blink.

"Archie, it's Dad," my father's voice says in my ear. "Pockets gave me an earpiece, too. He says this could be our only chance to get on a B.U.R.P. spaceship and learn their plans. You can use the force field, and of course we can be on board in less than a minute if you need us. Pockets already sprayed Camo-It-Now on the taxi and jammed B.U.R.P.'s radar so they won't know we're here." He lowers his voice and says, "Archie, this is a big deal, and if you're not ready for it, just say so. Honestly, I'm not ready for it, but I'm trying to be brave for the both of us."

I sort of want to cry, but I also really want to see inside a spaceship. I take a deep breath. "I'm ready."

The agent nods, assuming I'm speaking to him. He leads me toward a circle of white chalk a few feet away from us. The pouch with the plant in it bounces against my leg. I hope the Camo-It-Now doesn't wear off!

"After you," he says, motioning for me to step inside the circle. This seems like a very odd thing to do. Is a net going to spring up from the ground and trap me? I risk a quick glance up at the sky. I don't see the B.U.R.P. ship. Just a few puffy clouds. Maybe it's invisible, like the taxi.

"Go on," Pockets urges in my ear. Then, as though he knew what I'd been thinking, he adds, "It will be fine. I promise. Their ship is cloaked, too. No doubt for a quick mission like this, they only brought a small one. You'll look around for a few minutes, and then we'll come get you."

The agent gives me a gentle nudge toward the circle. The nudge, combined with the fact that I can now see a large pack of enormous black-and-gray dogs circling the base of the mountain, is enough to land me in the circle. The second both feet are inside, I feel a tingling that spreads up my body. For a moment I'm worried that whatever they're doing to me, it's going to cause my feet to stick to the ground, and those dogs seem like good climbers! They look more like wolves than dogs—not that a city kid like me has ever seen a real wolf. Still, they definitely don't look like they want to play fetch.

But it turns out that they are NOT trying to stick my feet to the ground. In fact, it's more like the exact opposite. With a *whoosh*, my feet lift off the ground, and I'm zooming up into the sky, right toward the largest, puffiest cloud! My hair whips around my head, and I quickly grab for my space map so it doesn't fly away. I hope that pouch is clipped on tight! I look down. The agent is zooming up below me. He looks bored, as though he does this every day.

I'm about to tell Pockets to rescue me RIGHT NOW and forget about the plan, when I suddenly shoot into the cloud. I'M IN A *CLOUD*! It is pretty much what you'd expect a cloud to be like—cold and wet and white. I tilt my head back and look up, which may have been a mistake, because now I know I'm heading right toward a huge metal object with GALACTIC painted across the bottom. All I can think to do is fling my arms over my head.

A few seconds later, a round hole appears in the bottom of the ship and I'm sucked inside. The floor instantly seals

beneath me. Going from zooming to standing throws me off balance, and I stumble backward, trying to catch my breath.

It's a good thing I moved, because the hole in the floor is back! The agent appears beside me—or, I should say, his *head* appears. The rest of him follows quickly behind. The floor closes up beneath him. He pats down his hair and adjusts his shirt.

"Well, that was something!" Dad's awed voice comes through my earpiece. "Pockets lent me the glasses. I felt like I was right there with you in that cloud! Gotta get me a pair of those!"

Now that I'm not terrified anymore, I realize it really WAS pretty cool!

"Come," the agent says. "You need to get back to your rooms. You can't very well show up to the meeting wearing *that*."

I'm a little insulted on behalf of my clothes, but I let his comment go.

The agent leads me through a series of long, narrow hallways lined with doors on one side and windows on the other. The windows show mostly a view of the cloud that hides the ship, but every once in a while I catch a glimpse of the sky and the mountainside. Pockets must have been wrong—this isn't a small ship. It's huge!

I don't see the taxi anywhere, which I know is how it's supposed to be. Then I remember I CAN see it. Well, the inside of it, at least! I can use the glasses! The agent has begun talking into a communication device on his wrist, so I slow down to widen the gap between us, then flick the switch.

And suddenly it's like I'm right there!

Pockets must have taken the glasses back, because I can see Dad in the driver's seat, tapping his fingers anxiously on the steering wheel. I want to shout, but I force myself to whisper. "Dad! I can see you!"

Dad jolts upright, his hand reaching for his earpiece. "Hey, Archie!" He reaches over to Pockets, and I can tell he's ruffling the fur on top of his head. I try not to laugh. Dad always used to ruffle my hair when I was little. Okay, sometimes he still does.

"Hey," Pockets grumbles. "Ask next time!"

Dad ignores him. "Son, I'm very proud of you. You're being very brave."

"Thanks, Dad," I whisper.

"We'll be right here with you," he says.

Then Pockets chimes in with, "Try to

explore as much of the ship as you can. I'm recording what you're seeing through your lenses."

I'm about to suggest hiding instead of exploring, when Pockets adds, "You'd better switch back now."

Dad gives a wave and I reluctantly turn the view back to the ship. It's a good thing I didn't wait much longer, because the agent has just stopped in front of a large wooden door and is waiting for me to catch up.

The door is much fancier than any we've passed so far. I don't see a doorknob or keyhole anywhere, though. The agent presses a nearly invisible button beside the door, and a keypad appears. He steps aside and gestures for me to use it. I look back at him blankly. He shakes his head. "Forgive me, but you'd forget your own birthday if it wasn't written down on one of those lists of yours," he says, punching in a series of numbers. The door slides into the wall with a nearly silent *swoosh*. "I will see you down in the laboratory in twenty minutes," he says, then turns and strides back in the direction we came from.

I stand in the hallway for a minute, not sure if I should go in or stay here. Voices headed my way from the end of the hall-way make my decision for me. I jump into the room. The door *swoosh*es closed behind me, plunging me into total darkness.

Why did I agree to this again?

CHAPTER SEVEN:
On Board the Mother Ship

I feel around the wall until I find a switch, but I don't turn the light on yet. What if the person whose room I'm in is waiting to jump out at me? Or the agent was tricking me and I'm actually in a jail cell? "Anytime now," Pockets nudges through the earpiece. Boy, he sure can be bossy, even long-distance!

I take a deep breath and flick the switch. The room lights up, and it's hands down the fanciest room I've ever seen outside of the movies or a magazine. Like five-star-hotel fancy. Like millionaire-movie-star fancy, with thick white carpets and gold statues and colorful paintings and shiny marble floors and tall columns with flowers and fruit bowls and glass cases filled with stuff I can't even identify from here. This one room is bigger than our whole apartment. Whoever that guard thinks my parents are, they must be very powerful and important people.

"Wow," Pockets says with a whistle.

"I know!" I reply. I rest my space map by

the door and take a few steps into the main part of the room. Up close, I can see that each glass case is filled with something weirder than the next. One has a sign with the words: THE LAST BOOGLER FISH. A large bowl of water sits inside the case. Swimming around the bowl is a tiny purple fish with long, floppy, bunny-like ears. I didn't even know fish *had* ears. "Hmm," Pockets says. "The boogler fish has been considered extinct for five years."

I move on to the next case. This one contains only a thin silver vase with a pink-and-white-striped flower sticking out. The sign reads: THE LAST LILANDRA FLOWER. A quick glance at the other cases tells me that each item—a leather-bound book, a metal coin, an animal horn—is the last of its kind.

THE LAST BOOGLER FISH

"I guess we know why B.U.R.P. wanted the plant," I tell Pockets. "Whoever lives here definitely likes to collect rare things."

"That's actually a relief," Pockets says. "Now at least we know B.U.R.P. wasn't after the plant as part of some sinister plot they were cooking up."

"Good! Then can you guys come pick me up now?"

"Soon," Pockets says. "You don't appear

to be in any danger, so would you mind taking a closer look around? See if you can find anything with the collector's name on it."

"Fine," I grumble. "But after this I want a raise."

"You're not even getting paid," Pockets points out.

"Then how about when I get back, you'll agree to come watch me play baseball?"

"Deal," he says. "Now go snoop around his desk. Try to find that list the agent mentioned."

I head toward a wide wooden desk piled high with papers. I spot a few computers and some gadgets that look a lot like ones I've seen Pockets use. "Hey," I say, picking up a force field pen. It says PROPERTY OF THE

ISF down the side! I pat my back pocket. Mine's still there.

"I knew it!" Pockets says. "B.U.R.P.'s been stealing our technology! That's how they always manage to stay one step ahead of us!"

I lift up the top sheet of paper and am about to peek at it, when I hear a low, wheezy sort of rumble. I freeze. It's quiet for few seconds, then I hear it again. It almost sounds like...

"Snoring!" Pockets, Dad, and I exclaim at the same time. I turn away from the desk, shoving the piece of paper into my pocket.

Behind me is the outline of a door. It blends into the wall so well I wouldn't have spotted it if not for the snoring coming from behind it. I tiptoe past the door, but I must have stepped too close, because it *whoosh*es open! Hasn't B.U.R.P. heard of *doorknobs*?!

The only light in the room is coming from glowing numbers projected on the wall, but I can still make out a few things. The huge bed in the center of the room is hard to miss, as is the boy-shaped lump under the blanket. At the bottom of the bed lies a small black cat. The boy-shaped lump is gently snoring. The cat-shaped lump is staring at me suspiciously with his greenish-gold cat eyes.

In my ear Pockets says, "Can you walk closer to the wall? I think it's a clock. I want to see how much time we have until he wakes up for the meeting at the laboratory."

"I'd really rather not," I whisper back. The cat is now sitting up, tilting his head at me. Something about the way he moves is familiar, but I don't have time to think about that now. The son of a clearly very important B.U.R.P. agent is about to wake up!

Two things happen at once. The cat lets out a loud meow right in my face as the numbers on the wall begin counting down: 59...58...57...56...

Something's going to happen in less than a minute! I'm pretty sure I don't want to be here when it does!

"We have to get to that meeting before he does!" Pockets says.

I'm more concerned with getting out of the room before he wakes up. I turn to run, but the cat springs up off the bed and jumps right at me!

I scramble backward and wind up directly at the foot of the bed. A beam of light suddenly shoots out from the wall and sweeps across my face. "Alarm off," a mechanical voice says.

The numbers on the wall disappear.

Oops! Someone is going to miss his meeting!

I run out of the room without looking back. Unfortunately, the cat has followed me out. I bend down to usher him back into the room before the boy wakes up and finds his cat gone. The cat won't budge. He just sits there, purring at me. I pick him up and move away from the door, which finally *whoosh*es closed behind me.

"Is that...?" Pockets begins. "It can't be....Is it?"

I squint at the cat. He really DOES seem familiar. At the sound of Pockets's voice in my earpiece, the cat squirms his way up my arm and nuzzles my ear! I gasp. "Pockets! This is the cat from the castle on Tri-Dark! The one who followed you around the castle on our last mission!"

"Yes, I believe it is," Pockets says. "And that means the boy in the bed is the same one who escaped from us!"

"You'd better not come on the ship or you might wind up his pet again!"

"Very funny," Pockets says.

The last time Pockets and I had seen this cat was in a castle on a planet far away from here. A boy whose face was hidden by the hood of his black cloak was feeding him and a bunch of other cats. The boy had taken a liking to Pockets, but Pockets was able to escape. I guess this other cat decided to stick around.

"What's important right now is that we get to that meeting," Pockets says. "We have to find the laboratory."

I grab my space map from where I'd left it by the front door. I pull it out of the tube and unroll it on the floor.

As I'd hoped, the whole floor plan of the B.U.R.P. ship rises into the air above my map. The ship is much bigger that I would have suspected, filled with rooms labeled with big words like CAFETERIA, MEDICAL BAY, LABORATORY, CONTROL ROOM, DOCKING BAY, RESEARCH AND DEVELOPMENT, and WEAPONS STORAGE, and many labeled PRIVATE, KEEP OUT.

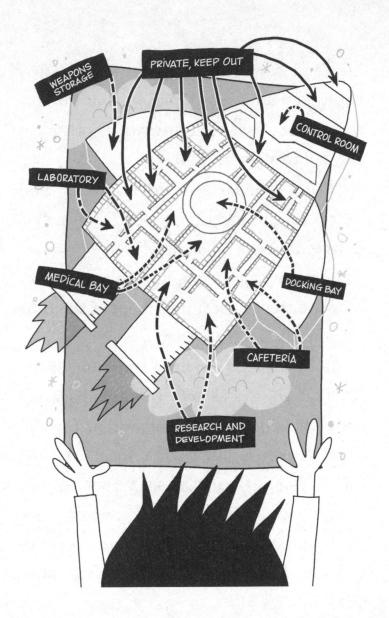

Pockets gasps. "Archie! This isn't just any B.U.R.P. ship you're on. This is the *mother ship*! The head of their whole fleet! Only the mother ship would have all those rooms!"

I try not to think of what any of that means and instead focus on finding the laboratory. "This is where I have to go," I tell Pockets, pointing to a room two flights down.

"Hurry," Pockets says. "The meeting is about to start. Whatever it's about is obviously important."

I quickly shove my map back into the case and at the last second remember I spotted a closet while searching for the light switch earlier. I rush over and root through the coats until I find what I'm looking for.

First, I tie the black cloak around my shoulders. Then I flip the hood up so it hangs over my face the same way the boy wore it when we spotted him on Tri-Dark.

I turn to face the full-length mirror inside the closet. "How do I look?" I ask Pockets.

"Like a fake vampire about to go trick-or-treating," he replies.

I peek out from under the hood. Hmm, he may be right. Still, just because that one B.U.R.P. agent might think all little boys look alike, it'll be safer to cover up. I don't know what happens to spies on the B.U.R.P. mother ship, and I don't want to find out.

CHapteR EiGHt:
Woof!

With the help of my space map and my vampire costume, I make it to the meeting without anyone stopping me. It might be my imagination, but whenever one of the crew passes by, it almost feels like they're bowing their heads at me. Then they rush off without making eye contact. It must be the cape. I'm pretty sure at home it wouldn't get the same reaction! People would think I was trying to be a super-hero. Guess all planets are different!

The laboratory looks like a more high-tech version of the science class in my elementary school, with tall tables and beakers and Bunsen burners. This one also has lots of computer equipment, cameras, lasers, and aliens. The B.U.R.P. aliens look mostly human, but with slight differences—larger eyes and heads, wider shoulders, and a little more hair than you'd normally see on arms and legs. But no one has three eyes or purple skin or scales or feathers, so I blend in well enough...for about five seconds, that is. That's when every single person in the room turns to face me. I cringe while I wait for them to ask who I am and what I'm doing here, but no one does. Instead, a woman with long red hair and a white lab coat steps forward. A label on her coat reads HEAD SCIENTIST, B.U.R.P.

"Sir," she says, "the team we sent to the surface to gather the canisantha will return in a moment. I will add it to the mixture and we can begin the experiment." She pauses, then asks, "Where is the black cat?"

The cat? I clear my throat. "Um... taking a nap? Or... washing his paws? He does that a lot."

The scientist sighs. "Sebastian, I know how much you like cats. But we need to test the potion. Once all the ISF agents on Friskopolus have been turned into wild dogs, they will finally leave us alone. We will be able to rule the universe without them constantly ruining our plans."

I hear Pockets shouting in my ear, but I can't make sense of what he is saying, because I'm trying to make sense of what *she's* saying. First off, she thinks I'm someone named Sebastian; second... they want to turn ISF agents into *dogs*? We were definitely wrong to assume this Sebastian person just wanted the plant for his collection of rare or extinct things.

On the other end of the earpiece, Pockets is still freaking out. Dad cuts in and says, "Pockets and I are on the way. Distract them until we arrive."

Great. How am I supposed to do that?

Turns out I don't have to do anything, because just then the real Sebastian walks into the room. He looks almost exactly like me. Or I look almost exactly like HIM. His head is a little bigger, and his arms are hairier and his nose is kind of off center, but other than that, we could be twins. He is holding the little black cat under one arm.

"I'm sorry I'm late," Sebastian says to the scientist. "I was certain I had set my alarm clock, but it never went off. Did I miss anything? Do you have the plant?" He waits for the woman to answer, and when she only stares back, Sebastian finally notices everyone else has gone silent, too. "What's going on?" he asks.

The head scientist points a shaky finger at me. Sebastian follows the finger, and his eyebrows shoot up. "Who are *you*?" he asks, stepping forward. Before I can react, he pulls off my sunglasses and pushes my hood back to fully reveal my face. My hair springs up. Sebastian gasps and drops the black cat.

"You...you look just like me!" he says.

Actually, I'm at least an inch taller, but I think it's best not to mention this.

He reaches his hand toward my face, and for a second I think he's going to hit me! But instead he just pinches my cheek to make sure I'm real. "You may have my face," he says, "but you cannot possibly be the equal of Sebastian the Great, the universe's most feared criminal mastermind, not to mention the founder and leader of B.U.R.P. So who *are* you?"

Sebastian the Great? That's the best nickname he could come up with?

Wait! Did he just say he's the *leader* of B.U.R.P.? But he's just a kid!

He is waiting for an answer, so I say, "Um, big criminal mastermind here, too. You know, trying to rule the universe and all."

Sebastian walks around me in a full circle, glaring. I cringe as he steps right on my sunglasses, snapping them in half. "There is only room for one of us," he says, hands on his hips. "What is the name of your organization?"

"Um, it's F.A.R.T.," I blurt out, then instantly wish I could take it back. It was all I could think of!

The boy frowns. "What does it stand for?"

"That is top secret information," I tell him in my best evil-mastermind voice. Clearly, I have no idea what it might stand for.

He nods in grudging approval. "Only a few know what B.U.R.P. stands for, and they are sworn to secrecy. Now, I demand you tell me what you are doing on my spaceship. It certainly looks like you are pretending to be me!"

Pockets whispers in my ear, "Stay calm. We're almost there."

I begin to explain that this is all a misunderstanding, when the door bursts open. Relief floods through me. Pockets and Dad have arrived!

Only it isn't Pockets and Dad. It's another scientist in a white lab coat— a man this time, with white hair and a cane made of gleaming black wood. He is followed by the agent who brought me to the ship. I shrink back a little, but the agent walks right past me.

"The canisantha is missing!" the new scientist tells Sebastian. "The plant was there this morning. Our team confirmed it with long-range photography. See?" He holds up a photograph that shows the plant I took. I don't dare glance down at my pouch.

"Are you certain you looked in the right spot?" Sebastian asks.

"Yes," he replies. "Absolutely."

"The dogs must have gotten to it,"

Sebastian says. "You promised me that the plant was secure up there."

"It was," the scientist insists. "The slope is too steep for the dogs to climb. That's why it had remained safe all these years. Plus, the plant was pulled up by the roots. So whatever—or whoever—took it must have known the roots were important."

"But no one left the ship," Sebastian says.

The agent steps forward. "Well, no one but you, sir," he says, almost apologetically. "You know, earlier. When you were wearing those odd clothes."

"You are mistaken," Sebastian says. "I've been taking a nap!"

The agent looks torn between wanting to argue and not wanting to accuse his boss of lying. He looks down at his feet. I slowly try to back up into the crowd. This would be a good time to disappear.

But it's too late. The agent looks up and spots me. He takes in my outfit and realizes I'm the one he saw, not Sebastian. He looks back and forth between the two of us, then cries out, "What? Who? Huh?" In an awkward attempt to reach for me, he crashes into a vat of bright pink liquid that the crowd was blocking before. The head scientist grabs it before it topples.

"Almost there," Pockets whispers in my ear.

Sure, I've heard *that* before.

The agent turns to Sebastian. "Is this some kind of trick? Is this a brother of yours?"

The B.U.R.P. leader shakes his head. "I assure you, I have never seen this boy before in my life."

The agent thrusts his finger in my face. "You were standing right by those plants! *You* took it and tricked me! Where is it?"

Before I can even think, the white-haired scientist begins waving his cane in a wide circle right in front of me. To my horror, my secret pouch with the missing plant is suddenly no longer so secret. They know how to dissolve Camo-It-Now! I quickly pull the cloak around me, but it's too late. I know they've seen it.

"Get out of there now!" Pockets shouts in my ear. I know he can't see me, since my glasses are broken on the floor, but what he can hear in the earpiece obviously has him worried. I wish we'd gotten to the martial arts part of our training, because bouncing a ball and skipping rope isn't going to help me right now. Before I can make a move, the agent grabs me by both arms.

Sebastian reaches into my pocket and pulls out the bag. His eyes light up. "We've got it!" he shouts. He hands it to the woman, who pulls the plant out of the bag and drops it into the vat. The plant sizzles, then sinks to the bottom. The mixture begins to darken. The other scientist scoops up the small black cat, who meows in protest.

"Is there no other way to test if the potion will work on talking cats?" Sebastian asks.

The head scientist shakes her head.

"We need to test it on a regular cat first. Then we will know the proper amount to feed our real target. Don't worry. It will be very painless, and it will last forever." She dips a pair of tongs into the vat and pulls off a piece of the plant no bigger than a pea. She reaches toward the cat's mouth.

"Not so fast," a familiar voice shouts.

It's Pockets! Dad is right behind him. Finally!

"Hey, I know you!" Sebastian shouts back. "You're that giant cat from the castle at Tri-Dark! But...you're talking! How is that...?"

Pockets whips out his ISF badge. "You are under arrest for stealing the last canisantha plant and planning evil deeds."

At the sound of Pockets's voice, the

little black cat's ears perk up. He tries to wriggle out of the scientist's arms, but for an old guy, the man is very strong.

The woman is now only a few inches from the little cat's mouth. Without taking time to think, I reach into my pocket and grab the force field pen. I aim it so that an invisible wall shoots up between the cat and the woman. She bumps right into it and snarls.

Sebastian calmly walks toward the wall and taps on it with his ring. The wall disappears. "Did you really think you could use one of your ISF gadgets on my ship and succeed?"

I swallow hard.

Sebastian plucks the pea-size ball from the woman's hand and walks right up to

Pockets. "We were going to test this on a wild cat first, but you would make a much better test subject."

I expect Pockets to go screaming from the room, but he holds his ground.

"Or..." Sebastian continues, "what if you come work for us instead? We could use a giant cat like you around."

Pockets shakes his head. "Trust me—I don't make a very good pet."

I don't want Pockets to stay here, of course, but I don't want him to eat that plant, either. "You make a great pet," I argue. "Penny's only talking now because of you."

Sebastian doesn't take his eyes off Pockets. "What's it going to be?" he asks. "Life as a highly respected member of

B.U.R.P. or a lifetime as a dog, your natural-born enemy?"

"I'll take the dog," Pockets says calmly. Then he plucks the ball from Sebastian's hand and brings his paw up to his own mouth! My jaw falls open!

The scientist was right—the change DOES happen fast! One second I'm looking at a giant white cat, and then his head changes and his tail spreads out and he's a green dragon! Then a second later he's a squirrel! Then a turtle. Then he turns into a dog that looks a lot like little Luna from back home. And finally, with a loud howl, he becomes one of the wild dogs from the planet below. My heart sinks when I look at him, but the B.U.R.P. people are cheering and high-fiving.

Their celebration is short-lived. The door *swoosh*es open, and a swarm of agents wearing ISF badges burst into the room and spread out. None, I notice, are cats. The B.U.R.P. members begin to shout and run. The ISF agents arrest everyone they can catch. The dog who was once Pockets hops from foot to foot and barks like the regular dog he is. My heart aches for him, and for us.

Then I notice that the old-man scientist is about to grab the vat of liquid on the lab table. Dad and I look at each other and, with a nod, hurry over to the table. Dad gets there first and sweeps the vat off the table. "NO!" both scientists cry as it crashes to the ground. Once the liquid spills out, the plant dissolves until nothing is left.

"Come, Archie," Dad says, yanking me toward the door. "We've got to try to catch Sebastian. He ran out!"

"But we can't leave Pockets! We have to do something!"

"Pockets has it under control," Dad says, pulling me down the hall. "You need to trust him."

I hesitate for a second, listening to the barking and shouting in the room we just left. Poor Pockets! It doesn't seem as though he's in control at all. What are we going to tell Penny when Pockets doesn't come home with us? He's become a part of our family.

The only thing that makes me feel better is that the ISF is here now, so they will make sure Pockets is taken care of. He won't be left in B.U.R.P.'s hands.

We make it out of the room and into the empty hallway. One glance out the window tells us we're too late to capture Sebastian. Looming in front of us is an oddly shaped space shuttle. Sebastian is sitting at the helm, steering away from the mother ship.

"That's his suite of rooms!" I exclaim, recognizing the bed and the huge desk and the collection of rare objects. "It must detach from the ship!"

"Come," Dad says, grabbing my hand. "Maybe we can catch him in the taxi."

We run to the docking bay where Dad parked. I look into the empty backseat as I climb in, my eyes filling with the tears I managed to hold in until now. Then I blink. It looked like something on the seat had shimmered for a second. I hear a little buzz, like a fly, and blink again.

"Took you guys long enough," Pockets says, suddenly appearing in the seat, looking every inch his old self: white fur, gray pockets, fluffy ears, big belly.

I jump so high I hit my head on the roof of the car! "What? How? Huh?" I realize Sebastian said almost the exact same thing when he first saw me, but I don't care. I scramble over the seat and squeeze Pockets into a big hug.

"Okay, okay," he says, pushing me away, "that's enough."

"But how did you do it?" I ask, wiping my tears away. "The scientist said the change would last forever."

"And maybe it would have," Pockets

says, "if I had actually eaten the plant." He grins and opens his paw to reveal the tiny ball.

My eyes widen. "But...but I saw you turn into a dog! And some other crazy creatures before that!"

He shakes his head. "Remember how I used my Atomic Assembler device to temporarily turn you and your father into aliens on our last mission? Well, what you saw in the lab was me using the Atomic Assembler to temporarily turn myself into a dog. After you two left the room, I turned myself into a fly and zoomed out of there! By the time the scientists realize they've been tricked, they'll have been arrested by the ISF. Then they'll have bigger problems than worrying where the dog went."

"I'm sorry I couldn't tell you, Archie," Dad says. "But we didn't know who may have been listening, so Pockets made me promise to keep his plan a secret until we were all safely back in the taxi."

"I'm just glad you're you!" I hug Pockets one more time and then climb into my own seat. "Now let's go get Sebastian!"

But to my surprise, Pockets says, "Not today. I was tracking his ship while I waited for you. Once it left the orbit of planet Canis, it disappeared from my radar. B.U.R.P. has a lot of technology that we don't. We'll find him someday, but for now, capturing the mother ship was a huge turning point in our efforts to bring down B.U.R.P. and keep the universe safe. Let's head home to celebrate."

"Say no more," Dad says, revving the engine. I strap in and get my map ready. The sun is setting as we soar over the gold-and-green mountaintops.

"It's too bad we don't know what Sebastian's plotting next," Dad says as the planet disappears out our back window.

"Wait! That reminds me!" I reach into my front pocket and pull out the crumpled piece of paper I'd taken from Sebastian's desk before I even knew who he was. It has the words LONG-RANGE PLANS TO RULE THE UNIVERSE printed at the top. I hand the paper to Pockets and say, "Looks like you're not the only one with surprises in his pockets. I have a feeling this will keep the ISF busy for a long time."

Pockets reads the list and beams at

me. "You've definitely earned yourself that raise," he says. He reaches over the seat to pat me on the head with his heavy paw.

"Wait a second," Dad says. "Archie's getting *paid*?"

Pockets and I laugh. "You're still coming to my baseball game, right?" I ask Pockets.

"Wouldn't miss it," he says.

"Hey, Pockets," Dad says. "Now that you've been a dog, it's not so bad, right? I think we're going to get one as a pet."

In response, Pockets turns himself back into a fly and burrows into the corner of the seat.

This time Dad and I laugh at Pockets. "I was only kidding," Dad says.

I turn to look at my map. I have to

prepare to guide us back through the Asteroid Belt. Sure, Sebastian's still out there, but tonight my whole family will be together. I can't think of a better reason to celebrate than that.

THREE SCiENCE Facts to IMPRESS YouR FRiENDS anD TeaCHERS

1. GREENHOUSES are glass buildings used by botanists (scientists who study plants), professional gardeners, and back-yard gardeners who may enjoy growing rare and exotic plants and flowers.

Sunlight passes through the glass walls of a greenhouse and is absorbed by the plants. The plants then give off their own heat, but that heat is unable to pass through the glass. This creates a warm environment and an even temperature in the greenhouse, allowing the plants to thrive. Greenhouses also protect plants from harsh elements like wind, rain, ice, and snow, and keep bugs and other animals away.

2. An animal or plant is considered **EXTINCT** when the last of the species is no longer alive. **EXTINCTION** happens for different reasons. Sometimes a particular animal is hunted too much, or a crop is overharvested. Sometimes forests are cut down, leaving animals without a home, or plants without the right environment to grow. Sometimes a new species is introduced into a habitat (a place where an animal or plant naturally lives or grows) and the existing animals can't compete.

Pollution in the air or water can also contribute to the extinction of a species. Thousands of animals and plants are on the ENDANGERED SPECIES LIST. This means there are so few of them left that it is illegal to harm them.

A MASS EXTINCTION happens when a large number of species become extinct at the same time. An asteroid caused the most recent mass-extinction event almost sixty-six million years ago. Three-quarters of all animal species, including all non-flying dinosaurs, became extinct.

3. An ASTEROID is a rock containing different types of metal. It orbits the sun, just as the planets do. But it is much, much smaller than a planet. In our solar system, the ASTEROID BELT orbits the sun between Mars and Jupiter. Scientists think it contains more than a million asteroids, ranging in size from a small pebble to a large country!

In the early days of our solar system, the planets were formed by gravity pulling dust and rocks together. Once Jupiter was formed, its strong gravity prevented a lot of those rocks from forming other planets; instead, the rocks were left to float around the sun. NASA currently has a spacecraft called DAWN exploring the largest asteroids in the Asteroid Belt in the hope of learning about life in the early formation of the solar system.

Whoever first discovers an asteroid gets to name it. Maybe one day an asteroid will be named after Archie or Pockets!

Don't miss a single **SPACE TAXI** adventure!

BOOK 1

BOOK 2

BOOK 3

BOOK 4